Enchantimals™

FELICITY FOX'S WILD WONDERWOOD ADVENTURE

ELLIE O'RYAN

LITTLE, BROWN AND COMPANY

New York Boston

Little, Brown and Company
Hachette Book Group
1290 Avenue of the Americas, New York, NY 10104
Visit us at lb-kids.com
enchantimals.com

First Edition: March 2018

Little, Brown and Company is a division of Hachette Book Group, Inc. The Little, Brown name and logo are trademarks of Hachette Book Group, Inc.

The publisher is not responsible for websites (or their content) that are not owned by the publisher.

Library of Congress Control Number 2017961336

ISBNs: 978-0-316-41371-8 (pbk.), 978-0-316-44865-9 (Scholastic ed.)

Printed in the United States of America

LSC-C

10 9 8 7 6 5 4 3 2 1

CHAPTER ONE

A SPECIAL DAY

Felicity stood back and stared at the massive pile of stuff in the middle of the room. The den where the fox-girl lived with her bestie, Flick, was snug and cozy. But the size of the pile made it seem smaller than ever!

"What do you think, Flick?" she asked. "Is that *everything* we need? Did we forget anything?"

There was no answer.

"I just don't want to forget something really important," Felicity continued. "Once you're in the wilderness, you can't

1

just stop by a store. You either improvise or you go without. Know what I mean?"

Flick still didn't respond.

Felicity paused. "Flick?" she called out. "Where are you?"

She stood very still, listening with all her might. Her pointed fox ears quivered as they tried to pick up the slightest sound. Then Felicity heard it: a faint *scritch-scratch-scritch* that could only be one thing. Flick was digging! Flick's little black paws had strong claws that were perfect for digging holes, tunnels, and burrows.

But why would Flick be burrowing *inside* their cozy little den?

Suddenly, Felicity's hands flew to her face as she gasped. "Flick! Are you digging out of the camping gear?" she exclaimed.

Scritch-scratch! Scratch-scritch!

The sound was coming from inside the pile of camping supplies.

Felicity's guess was correct!

"Don't worry, Flick!" she cried. "I'm on my way!"

The mess kit. The map. The compass. The canteen. Soon they were all flying through the air as Felicity tore through the pile to reach her bestie. At last, she saw it: Flick's small paw poking out of the pile.

"Gotcha!" Felicity exclaimed as she grabbed Flick's paw and pulled, pulled, *pulled* until Flick popped out of the pile. Felicity and Flick flew back and tumbled across the floor, finally coming to a landing on a soft, squishy stack of sleeping bags.

Felicity and Flick waggled their ears together, which was their special way of showing affection for each other.

"I'm sorry, Flick! I guess I got a little carried away with my packing. I didn't mean to cover you with all this stuff!"

"Uh-huh-huh!" Flick replied, letting Felicity know she forgave her.

"It's just that—well, you know—we've been planning this camping trip for ages and ages, and I want everything to be just right!"

Flick looked carefully at the humongous pile of supplies. "Doo ma stoo!"

"You're right; we *do* have way too much stuff!" Felicity said with a giggle. "Let's split this stuff into two piles—one for things we really need to take, and one for things we can leave at home."

Soon they had a more manageable pile of things to bring. Felicity's hand hovered over a bright blue box as she wondered whether she should bring it. *I don't think we'll need any of this stuff*, she thought. *But I'd hate to need it and not have it.*

Felicity nodded to herself and placed the blue box on the top of the to-bring pile.

"Much better," she announced. "I don't know what I was thinking with all that stuff. We'd have to spend the entire day carting it to our campsite! And I don't know about you, Flick, but I'd *much* rather have an adventure with our friends!"

Flick was about to respond when, suddenly, there was a knock at the door. "Did you hear that, Flick?" Felicity asked, her eyes shining happily. "It must be one of our friends. And that means adventure starts...*now!*"

CHAPTER TWO

THE WEATHER KNOWER

Felicity ran over to the door and opened it. Her friend Danessa the deer-girl was standing on the doorstep with her bestie, a deer named Sprint! Danessa smiled up at Felicity from under her floppy-brimmed hat. It was open at the top to make room for Danessa's curved antlers.

"I should've known you two would be the first to arrive!" Felicity said with a laugh. "Did you run all the way here?"

"How'd you guess?" Danessa replied.

"It's a beautiful morning for a race, right, Sprint?"

"Ya ya," Sprint agreed.

"It's perfect camping weather, too," Felicity added. "Not too hot, not too cold, nice and sunny. I can't wait to get started. I have so many fun adventures planned!"

Danessa and Sprint touched their antlers together in excitement. "We can't wait, either," Danessa said. "We've never been camping before."

"Flick and I have it all planned out," Felicity replied. "We'll have two tremendous days jam-packed with adventure! I found the perfect camping site—it's in a clearing in the cherry grove, so I think we'll have a terrific view of the night sky. We might even be able to see shooting stars! Best of all, though, there's a brand-new trail...one I've never, ever seen before! As soon as I saw it, I just knew it would be the perfect adventure for our big camping trip. I was *so* tempted to start exploring it right away...but I knew it would be even better to wait for all of you!"

Flick's nose twitched. "Foo fwa!" she said, tugging on Felicity's hand. Felicity turned around to see Sage and her bestie, Caper, strolling down the path. Even if Felicity hadn't seen Sage, she would've known she was near from the scent of Sage's special perfume. The skunk-girl wore it every day.

As Felicity and Flick greeted Sage and Caper, some bright purple and teal feathers appeared in the distance. That could only mean one thing: Patter the peacock-girl and her bestie, Flap, were on their way, too!

Felicity gave a big wave so Patter could see her. "Hi, Patter! Hi, Flap!" she called.

"It's finally here!" Patter sang out. "The camping trip we've been waiting for! Flap and I are *sooo* excited!"

"It's here—but where are Bree and Twist?" Felicity asked. She stood on tiptoes to peer over her friends' heads. "You don't think they forgot...do you?"

"Forgot? How could they forget?" Sage teased Felicity. "It's all you've been talking about for weeks! Maybe they are playing a prank and trying to make you think they forgot!"

"Bla do gee!" Caper said with a giggle.

"You're right, Caper!" Sage said, "high-fiving" her bestie's tail with her own. "That *does* sound more like something we would do!"

9

Everyone laughed—especially Felicity. But as their laughter faded, Felicity started to look worried. "Do you think they got confused about the day?" she said. "What if Bree thinks the camping trip starts tomorrow?"

"Don't worry," Patter assured her. "Bree is probably just caught up in one of her inventions. I can't imagine that she'd forget...or get the day wrong..."

"I have an idea," Sage said suddenly. "What are we waiting around for? If Bree's not here, let's go over to her house and find out what's going on. What do you think?"

"That's music to my ears!" Patter trilled.

"Why didn't I think of that?" Felicity exclaimed. "Let's go!"

The friends hurried along the path, where golden sunlight filtered through the fluttering leaves. Felicity shivered a little, but not because she was cold. No, it was because the whole world seemed to be holding its breath, as if something special—something incredible—something *big!* was about to happen.

In a few minutes, the friends arrived at Bree's cozy cottage. They found her standing in the front yard, frowning at a strange device in her hands. Her bestie, Twist, was perched on her hind legs. Her nose twitched wildly as she sniffed the unusual object.

"Bree! Good morning!" Felicity cried. "What are you doing?"

Bree looked up, surprised. "Oh! Hi, everybody! What are you doing here?" she asked. "Oh no—the camping trip—we're late? I must be *so* late! I'm sorry!"

"Don't worry about it," Felicity said, secretly glad to learn that Bree hadn't forgotten after all. "We were just wondering where you were—"

"And if you need any help getting ready or packing or anything at all?" Danessa interrupted.

"I do need some help," Bree admitted. "But...I don't exactly know *what* kind of help I need."

Felicity's curiosity was piqued. Her pointy ears twitched, alert and ready to hear more.

"Why don't you tell us all about it?" Patter suggested. "I'm sure we can figure it out together!"

"Thanks," Bree said. She held out the device. "Want to take a look?"

Sage reached for it first. "What *is* this thing?" she asked. Caper was by her side in an instant, looking at the instrument just as closely as her bestie. It was made of a slender metal tube that felt cool in her hands. A sparkly green liquid flowed through the tube as Felicity turned it back and forth. At each end of the tube was a delicate glass bulb. "Oh, let me guess. You built this, didn't you?"

"Yup," Bree replied, nodding her head. "It's a Weather Knower, which is a fancy name for a tool that can help predict the weather. I got the idea a week ago—I thought, *Wow, wouldn't it be cool if we knew what the weather would be like for our camping trip?* Then we could pack less, and *unpack* less, which means—"

"Getting to the fun faster," finished

Sage for her. She and Caper high-fived their tails.

"Exactly!" Bree said. "So Twist and I went right to work. It's actually pretty simple...and really cool....The pressure in the air changes depending on what kind of weather is coming. Low pressure means a storm is on the way. It makes the liquid go *down, down, down*—and light up the blue bulb. High pressure, or no storms coming, will make the liquid go *up, up, up*—and light up the gold bulb. Make sense?"

Felicity, Sage, Danessa, and Patter all nodded.

"It's an awesome invention," Patter said. "Can we try it?"

"To da do!" Twist said, hopping around impatiently.

"Exactly, Twist!" Bree nodded. "You

see, that's the tricky part. I *thought* it worked great. It predicted the weather accurately for five days in a row."

"So what's the problem?" asked Sage.

"Watch this," Bree said. She took the Weather Knower back from Felicity and held it very still. The friends watched in silence as the green liquid dropped through the tube—and the glass bulb glowed blue.

"The blue light?" Felicity asked in surprise, her ears quivering. "That's the one that means a storm, right?"

Bree nodded.

"But the sun is shining!" Felicity said.

"No ag boo!" Flick agreed.

"I know! There aren't any signs of a storm at all," Bree agreed. "So...what's wrong with my Weather Knower?"

There was a long silence as everyone thought about it.

"Do you think it really might start to rain?" Danessa asked gently.

"No ray!" Sprint said worriedly.

"It *can't* rain," Felicity said firmly. "The weather is *perfect*—just as it was yesterday, and the day before yesterday, and the day before the day before yesterday—"

"It hasn't rained in days and days and days," Patter added.

"Phew la!" Sprint said happily.

"I'm sure you're right," Bree responded. "Too bad about my Weather Knower. Hopefully a few adjustments will make it start working again."

"If anybody can figure out how to fix it, it's you and Twist!" Patter said encouragingly.

Felicity picked up Bree's knapsack. "What do you think?" she asked. "Ready to go?"

Bree grinned at her as she reached for the knapsack. "You bet!" she replied. "All set—right, Twist?"

"Ya go!" Twist agreed, stamping her foot excitedly.

Bree slipped the broken Weather Knower into one of the pockets and tried not to think about it.

CHAPTER THREE

THE PERFECT CAMPSITE

After a quick stop at Felicity's den for everyone else's camping gear, the friends were at last ready for their trip to begin! As Felicity led them along the twisty path to the campsite, their excited chatter almost drowned out the birds twittering in the trees—almost.

"I have so many incredible adventures planned for us!" Felicity said. "And lots of little surprises, too! The first one is our campsite—oh, just wait until you see it!

18

The spot we chose is just *purr*fect for us to set up our tents, but that's all I'm telling you for now!"

"Aw, come on, Felicity, can't you give us a little hint?" asked Sage, scampering from one side of the path to the other.

"But a hint might ruin the surprise!" Felicity replied.

"Hint! Hint!" Caper cheered, clapping her paws excitedly.

"Pleeeeeeease?" chorused her friends.

Felicity thought about it for a moment. "Sorry," she finally said. "But the good news is we're almost there! Everybody, grab hands and close your eyes."

"Hey! I can't see where I'm going!" Sage complained. "What if I walk into a tree? Or trip over a rock?"

"That's why we're holding hands,"

Danessa explained. "So we can guide one another."

"Don't worry," Felicity assured them. "I'm looking out for you! Just a few steps more...almost there now..."

Felicity dashed ahead to pull aside the thick canopy of vines so her friends wouldn't accidentally walk into it. "Surprise!" she cried. "You can open your eyes now!"

Felicity stood back and watched proudly as her friends got their very first glimpse of the campsite. The huge clearing was the perfect space for each girl and her bestie to pitch whatever kind of tent they wanted to camp in.

"Ta-da!" Flick announced proudly, her smile as big as Felicity's.

Felicity glanced around the campsite, seeing it for the first time through her friends' eyes. The friends *ooh*ed and *ahh*ed over the magnificent space and got to work immediately. Within no time, each girl and her bestie had set up their perfect tent....

There was Patter and Flap's tent, indigo and purple with sparkly gold fringe... and next to that, Bree and Twist's tent, pink with potted carrots in front so Twist could have a little snack to nibble whenever she got hungry. Then came Danessa and Sprint's tent: soft fabric covered with a wildflower pattern. It was crowned with sticks and twigs that looked remarkably like Danessa's and Sprint's antlers. After that was Sage and Caper's tent—striped, of course, just like Sage's and Caper's bushy tails! Felicity and Flick's own tent had a rounded dome for the top, just like their den back home.

"This looks incredible!" Felicity exclaimed as she took in her friends' tents.

"Yay yay a!" Flick agreed.

Felicity pointed upward with a grin. "You know what we'll see later, after it gets dark?" she asked. "Shooting stars! I'm sure of it!"

"Really?" Bree gasped in excitement.

"This is going to be the most amazing camping trip ever!" Patter agreed, fluttering off the ground in excitement, Flap by her side.

"Yay! I'm so glad you like the campsite!" Felicity cried. "Wait until you find out what we're going to do next!"

She skipped over to the largest rock and spread out a map that she and Flick had spent hours creating. The friends crowded around, each one trying to get a better look.

"La da!" Caper cried.

"That's right!" Sage exclaimed. "That's our campsite, isn't it?"

Felicity nodded enthusiastically. "You got it!"

"This map is really cool," Sage said.

"There's just one problem," Felicity said, her eyes twinkling.

"What's the problem?" asked Danessa, immediately concerned.

"I haven't been able to finish it!" Felicity exclaimed. She swept her paw over one side of the map, which was still blank. "Can you guess why?"

"Because you were so busy having adventures?" Sage asked.

Felicity shook her head.

"Because you were so busy choosing our incredible campsite?" guessed Danessa.

"Nope!" Felicity replied. "It's because I don't know what's over there. *No one does.*"

A hush fell over the group.

"Wha wha?" Flap asked, worriedly. Patter cuddled her bestie to comfort him.

Felicity just smiled mysteriously. "Follow me," she replied.

"Tha way," Flick added.

The duo crept through the clearing with their friends right behind them. On the opposite side, Felicity paused. "Watch this," she told the group. She wasn't sure why her voice had dropped to a whisper. Maybe because everything felt so mysterious... and the chance for adventure was so enormous....

The ivy was thick between the two trees, forming a dark green curtain of dense, shiny leaves. Felicity carefully patted it until she found what she was looking for—two loose vines that were easy to pull apart. She separated the curtain of ivy to reveal...

A twisty, turny path! Beams of golden sunlight sparkled down on the path, which was flecked with pretty pebbles and sparkly chips of mica. The path was made of deep, rich dirt; it was loose and soft, since no one had been trampling on the secret trail.

"In all the times I've explored Everwilde, I've never, ever seen this path before," Felicity said. "I have no idea where it leads...or what we might find there...."

"Maybe a new flower!" exclaimed Sage, excitedly high-fiving her tail with Caper's.

"Maybe a new waterfall!" said Bree, dancing happily with Twist.

"Or maybe a new friend!" Danessa

added. Sprint nuzzled Danessa with his antlers.

"Maybe!" Felicity said, wiggling her ears in excitement. "But one thing I know for sure is that it will be a big adventure... and I can't wait to find out!"

Patter clapped her hands together. "Can we go right now?" she asked.

"Soon," Felicity promised. "First, I thought we could hike all the way to the tippity-top of Whimsy Peak Mountain. Since it's the tallest mountain in Everwilde, the view will be incredible, and if we leave now, we won't have to hike up there during the hottest part of the day."

Flap's feathers fluttered nervously.

"Is it very, very, very high?" Sage asked. "With a steep cliff and a sharp drop?"

"Well...kind of—" Felicity started to say.

Patter quickly interrupted. "But not *too* high," she assured Flap. "Or too steep or too sharp."

Flap still looked a little nervous, so Patter smiled encouragingly at her bestie. "I know we don't love to fly too high, Flap, but we can do this! Besides, we'll be with our friends, and together we can do anything! Why don't we take a short practice flight together?"

Flap's feathers fluttered some more, but he looked more confident after his bestie's pep talk. "Ya we go," he replied.

All their friends cheered as Patter and Flap took flight! Moments later, they glided to a stop several feet away, Flap beaming with happiness. "You did it!" Patter exclaimed. "That wasn't so bad, was it?"

At that moment, a long shadow crept over the clearing. All the colors seemed to droop in the sudden gloom.

Felicity craned her neck to look at the sky. To her surprise, a thick cloud had blown across the sun.

And it wasn't the only one. Other heavy gray clouds were moving on the breeze, too.

Where'd those clouds come from? Felicity wondered. The sky had been so clear that morning.

"Uh-oh."

Bree's voice sliced through Felicity's thoughts. She turned to look at Bree, to ask her what was wrong.

But Felicity didn't need to ask. One

glance at Bree told her everything she needed to know.

Bree was standing in the center of the clearing, holding her Weather Knower. This time, though, the blue bulb on the end wasn't just lit.

It was flashing!

CHAPTER FOUR

TO THE TOP OF THE MOUNTAIN

W hat—what's that supposed to mean?"
Felicity asked.

"Well, it's never done that before," Bree
began, hopping nervously from foot to foot,
"but if my calculations are correct, and all
the settings are properly calibrated..."

"Go on," Sage urged her.

"It means rain is *definitely* on the way,"
Bree finally said. "I'm sorry, Felicity."

Felicity tried to laugh it off. "On the

way," she repeated. "That doesn't mean it's here yet! Or even that it's going to rain today. Come on! We can still hike to the top of Whimsy Peak! Race you!"

Danessa and Sprint couldn't resist an offer like that. "On your mark get set *go*!" Danessa said, all in a rush. The friends grabbed their knapsacks and took off, giggling as they flew, hopped, and scampered over the forest path.

Felicity paused only long enough for a last glance back at the secret path. *Not much longer*, she told herself.

Then she took off running as fast as she could!

Felicity and Flick were so familiar with the trail that they could've run to the top of the mountain blindfolded and never missed a step. They easily passed their friends, who had to keep a careful eye on the trail to avoid tripping over a tree root or stumbling on a loose stone. But Felicity wasn't interested in winning a last-minute race with her friends. She slowed down and waited for everyone else to catch up.

"That was fun!" Felicity said excitedly, waggling her ears together with Flick's.

"You know what would be really fun?" asked Danessa. "Relay races! Those are fawntastic because everybody on the team gets to win."

"*Oooh*, how about a relay race with a tricky obstacle course?" suggested Sage.

"Trick! Trick!" Caper exclaimed happily.

Felicity's eyes lit up. "I love it!" she cried. "Maybe we can build one tomorrow.

The forest is full of things that make excellent obstacles...boulders and hollow logs and tangly vines..."

"And prickly burrs," Patter said as she plucked one from her tail feathers. "*Yowch!* Watch out for the brambles."

"Don't forget jumping over streams," Danessa said with a graceful leap.

"I just had the most awesome idea!" Felicity exclaimed. "When we explore the secret path later, we can keep an eye out for obstacles."

"And turn the secret path into an obstacle course!" Sage added.

"Trick, trick!" Caper exclaimed again.

"That's right!" Sage laughed. "We'll make sure to make the obstacles *extra* tricky!"

Felicity was so excited, she scampered

ahead a little ways and jumped onto a heavy boulder by the side of the trail, Flick right by her side. The two besties happily nuzzled their ears together once again. Everything was working out even better than Felicity had hoped! Her friends had pitched pawsome tents, they were just as excited about the secret path as she was, and best of all, they had tons of ideas for how to make their camping trip even more fun and exciting.

"You know what? I think even the weather is working out *purr*fectly," Felicity declared. "Those clouds are keeping it nice and cool, so we can run as much as we want without getting too hot. It's like getting to have an adventure *and* spend the whole day under a shady tree."

"It's definitely cooler than it was this morning," Danessa agreed.

"The wind's really picking up, too," added Bree as it flattened her long ears.

"Patter, is this what it feels like to fly?" asked Sage, stretching her arms out wide.

"A little!" Patter said with a giggle.

"Fweeee!" Flap agreed. Flap was hopping and gliding alongside the group. He seemed to have forgotten that, just a few minutes ago, he'd been a little afraid to fly so high up. Now he knew it wasn't scary at all!

"I bet it would feel even more like flying if we ran—with the wind at our backs," Danessa said. "Anyone up for another race?"

"Now, now!" Sprint cheered.

"The top of the mountain's not far!" Felicity exclaimed. "If we run, we'll get there even faster!"

"Let's do it!" Bree cheered.

The friends' footsteps echoed along the trail as they picked up speed, and the wind carried their excited laughter high into the sky. Felicity was glad that Danessa had suggested running again. She thought her friends might not notice the last, extra-steep part of the path before they arrived at the mountaintop, where tall grasses and flowers in every color of the rainbow grew.

Felicity craned her neck to look up at the last part of the trail. "Just a few more minutes until we reach the top," she called to her friends. "You won't believe the view! It's one of the most—*ahhhh!*"

"Felicity! What's wrong?" Danessa cried.

Felicity had come to a complete stop, her hand over her eye. "N-nothing," she said. "I got something in my eye, that's all. It just surprised me."

"Here, let me take a look," Danessa offered. "Do you think it was a bug?"

"Um, no, actually," Felicity replied. "I think...I think it was a raindrop."

Her friends were quiet.

"It didn't really hurt," she said. "I just... wasn't expecting it."

Plink!

"I think I felt one!" Patter cried, folding her tail feathers around her shoulders like a shawl.

Plink!

"That's another—*oof*," Danessa added just as Sprint shivered beside her. She whispered, "Don't worry, Sprint," to her bestie. "It's just a few raindrops."

Plink!

The next raindrop bounced right off Twist's twitchy nose, making everybody giggle!

Then Danessa turned to the group. "Here's an idea. Sprint and I will race back to the campsite to see if everything is staying dry. Maybe we're just under a little rain cloud up here."

Plink!

"Yeah!" Bree said. "It's possible that everything is dry and cozy back at our campsite."

"Back soon with a full report," Danessa promised.

Plink!

"Wait!" Felicity cried. But it was too late. Danessa and Sprint had already dashed down the trail. They were so fast that they had already disappeared behind the bend in the path, and Felicity couldn't even see them anymore.

Felicity sighed. "They didn't need to go all the way back to the campsite," she explained to the others. "We're almost at the top of the mountain—up there, we'll be able to see what the weather is like all over Everwilde."

Plink, plink, plink!

Patter shivered as the raindrops drenched her glamorous updo. "Let's go see, then," she said. "And let's hurry!"

"Go, go!" Flap agreed.

There wasn't much laughter as Bree,

Felicity, Sage, Patter, and their besties finished their trek to the top of the mountain. Felicity didn't want to believe it, but it seemed as if the rain was picking up. Still, she crossed her fingers and hoped as hard as she could that they would see clear skies when they reached the mountaintop.

"Almost there!" she called to her friends, making her voice sound even more cheerful than usual. "It's just...over...this...ridge!"

The meadow, though, was not what Felicity had expected. It looked so different. Had it changed somehow?

Then she realized that all the flowers were closed tight, their petals curled up against the raindrops that were falling more and more steadily. The wind was blowing stronger, bending all those tall, delicate grasses nearly in half. The biggest change, though, was the light. The sun was completely blocked by the clouds, and all the bright, vibrant colors that Felicity remembered looked as if they had faded.

She glanced over at her friends, wanting to apologize. But to Felicity's surprise, they were wide-eyed with wonder.

"What a gorgeous meadow!" Bree cried.

"Too bad Danessa isn't here to see it," Patter remarked. "She and Sprint would already be racing through the grass!"

"If you think this is great, you really should see it when the sun is shining," Felicity said. "It's really incredible. In the sunlight, I mean."

Sage peered up at the sky. "Don't think that will be this trip, though," she replied. "Because all I can see is clouds. Clouds and clouds and clouds and clouds."

"Clow, clow, clow," Caper repeated.

It was true. A thick canopy of clouds had blown in on the wind, and they completely covered all of Everwilde.

"Usually you can see for miles and miles," Felicity said, her voice tinged with sadness.

Bree tilted her head, squinting as she stared into the distance. "See those silvery streaks?" she suddenly exclaimed. "I think that's rain pouring down over Wonderwood!"

"I think you're right," Patter agreed. "It's not raining nearly as hard up here, though."

"Do you think the storm already passed over this part of Everwilde?" Sage asked. "We would've noticed it...right?"

"We'll know which way the storm is

heading by the direction of the wind," Bree explained. She pointed to a leaf hanging from a tree branch, watching it sway in the wind. "You can tell the direction the wind is coming from by looking at the leaf," she explained to her friends.

"Really?" Patter asked anxiously. "How long until it gets here?"

Please say tomorrow. Please say tomorrow, Felicity thought.

"I don't know the answer to that question," Bree replied. "It all depends on the speed of the wind. I can't calculate the exact speed of the wind with just this leaf, but it does seem to be moving pretty fast…"

"From where da!" Twist added excitedly, hopping up and down to catch Bree's attention.

"That's right, Twist." She nodded. "The

direction is just as big a puzzle piece. If the wind changes, the storm could head over to a completely different part of Everwilde."

"You really think that could happen?" Felicity asked hopefully.

"Anything's possible," Bree began. "But—"

A low rumble of thunder interrupted her words. All the girls knew it wasn't a good sign.

"Maybe...maybe we should get back to our tents," Patter said.

"Okay," Felicity said, nodding her head. She wasn't that worried about the silvery streaks of rain in the distance—or even the rumbling thunder. After all, even after she and Flick had decided what to leave behind, Felicity had tried to prepare for everything. She remembered the special blue box and smiled to herself. *All we have to do is get back to our campsite,* she told herself. *Then we'll get this trip back on track.*

Thunder rumbled again—louder this time. Flick nudged Felicity's hand with a strange urgency. "Ahh-ackkk!"

"Okay," Felicity whispered near her ear. "We'll get going." In a louder voice, she said to her friends, "It will be even quicker to get back to our campsite. Downhill is so much easier than up—"

Crack!

A blindingly bright bolt of lightning tore through the sky! Its jagged forks ripped through the purple clouds, which dropped torrents of rain on the meadow. It was the biggest rainstorm any of them had ever seen, and there was only one thing to do.

Run!

CHAPTER FIVE

RAIN, RAIN, GO AWAY!

The heavy rain pelted their backs and drenched their hair as the girls scurried down the mountain, holding on to one another to keep from slipping on the slick trail. Their animal besties were soaking wet, too. Even though Flap had decided flying high up on the mountain wasn't so bad after all, his wings were too soggy to fly. He perched on Patter's shoulder to avoid the puddles, which slowed his

bestie down as she tried to rush down the
mountain.

Caper's and Flick's wet fur dragged
in the mud, which was so thick that poor
Twist's back paws kept getting stuck.

"Jump up," Bree said, holding her arms
open wide for Twist after she realized Flap
was hitching a ride with his bestie. The
quicker they could all get to the campsite,
the better! Soon Felicity and Sage were
carrying their besties, too.

"Not much longer now," Felicity told
them. She wanted to tell her friends that
everything would be better as soon as they
reached the campsite—she'd planned for
everything, after all—but the rain was
pounding so loud that it would've drowned
out her voice. *Better to get back to camp and*

out of the storm first, Felicity thought. Soon enough, her friends would be warm, dry, and comfortable. Felicity would make sure of that.

One tent glowed with light through the dim gloom of the storm when Felicity and the others finally reached the campsite. Danessa and Sprint were standing just under the tent's canopy, peering anxiously into the storm. When Danessa spotted Felicity and the others, a wave of relief flooded her face.

"Oh! You're back! We're so glad!" Danessa cried out. She held the flap of the tent open as wide as she could and called, "Come in! Hurry! Hurry!"

The others zipped over to Danessa and Sprint's tent, but Felicity and Flick veered off in a different direction. "Be right there!" she yelled over her shoulder. In her own tent, Felicity started searching, tossing cookware and pillows through the air.

"Do you see it, Flick?" she asked. "I *know* we brought it—the emergency box—it's got to be here somewhere!"

"*Feee!* Lookee!" Flick said, holding the box above her head.

"Oops," Felicity said with a giggle. "Was it right there the whole time?"

Flick nodded.

"Thanks, friend," Felicity said, waggling ears with her bestie. "What would I do without you? Come on, let's go join the others."

Felicity hoisted the heavy box into her arms and hurried over to the entrance. At the edge of their tent, though, Flick paused.

"Come on," Felicity repeated. "Everyone's waiting for us."

But Flick had an idea. She dove into the emergency supply box Felicity held and emerged a moment later, holding a bright blue poncho.

"Great idea!" Felicity exclaimed. The poncho was quite large, so Felicity cradled Flick in the crook of her arm and zipped up the poncho over them. Then she dashed into the storm, dodging the pelting raindrops as best she could. As soon as they reached Danessa's tent, Sprint and Danessa held open the entrance to let them in.

"Where did you go?" Sage demanded. "One minute you were right behind me, the next minute—*poof!* Gone!"

Felicity shrugged off the dripping poncho. "Sorry," she replied. "Flick and I wanted to get a few supplies from our own tent. The storm may have taken us by surprise today, but we tried our best to plan for everything—even weather that wouldn't cooperate!"

Felicity placed the blue box on the ground and eased off the top. "Ta-da!" she said proudly. "Ponchos for everyone to keep us dry from raindrops and drips. Hot cocoa mix for warming up. And I've got lots of snacks, too—trail mix and crunchy apples and all the fixings for yummy s'mores, too!"

"S'mores? My favorite!" Sage cheered.

Felicity's smile faltered for a moment. "Except…I forgot about building a campfire," she said. "We won't be able to get a fire started until the rain stops."

"Maybe we could try cold s'mores," Patter suggested.

"You ca do, la la!" Twist said to Bree.

"Aw, thanks for the vote of confidence!" Bree replied to her bestie. "I probably *could* invent a way to roast the marshmallows inside, but not from this tent. Cold s'mores sound pretty good though. Maybe we can add carrots to ours!"

"Maybe," Felicity said, but her voice was full of doubt. After all, half the fun of eating s'mores was toasting the marshmallows . . . and the other half was the way the gooey marshmallows made the chocolate melt. "Well, anyway, hopefully the rain will clear up by evening and—"

"*Oh no!*" Flick exclaimed suddenly.

"What? What's wrong?" all the friends exclaimed.

Felicity realized exactly what was wrong as she turned to Flick with a look of dread on her face. "The firewood—you didn't happen to put a tarp over it or anything, did you?"

Flick shook her head and looked down at the ground, ashamed.

"No, no, it's not your fault," Felicity assured her. "I should've remembered. I was just so excited...and there was so much to do....I can't believe I forgot!"

"You forgot the firewood back home?" Patter asked, trying to figure out why Felicity was so upset.

"I wish," Felicity said ruefully. "No, it's even worse. I remembered the firewood, but I forgot to cover it! Now it's going to be completely soaked, and even if the rain stops, we won't be able to have a campfire!"

"So...no toasty-hot s'mores," Danessa said. "That's okay! We can eat them cold...with carrots, like Bree said!"

"But no toasty-hot dinner, either," Felicity said. "We won't have a place to warm up or tell stories or sing songs. I ruined our camping trip."

"Hey, don't talk like that!" Patter said. "It was just an accident."

"An easy mistake," Bree added. "Any one of us could've made it."

"Ex-ex-exactly," Sage said, her teeth chattering. She shivered as she twisted water out of her long, bushy tail.

"Well, at least we have the ponchos," Felicity said, trying to look on the bright side. "They'll keep us from getting even wetter!"

Flick passed out ponchos to each friend and her animal bestie.

"Who wants some trail mix?" Felicity asked as everyone pulled on their ponchos.

Suddenly, Danessa leaped to her feet. "Whoa! Why am I sitting in a puddle?" she cried. "Sage—are you pranking me?"

"Not this time," Sage replied. "I think we're all wet enough. We wouldn't do that—right, Caper?"

"No, no," Caper agreed.

"Was it a leak?" Felicity asked, staring up at the top of the tent. The canopy was supposed to be waterproof…and the roof certainly looked dry….

Bree scrambled up and started to investigate. *"Hmm,"* she said to herself. Then she poked her head outside. "Oh. Uh-huh. *Ahhh.* Yes, of course."

"Of course what?" Felicity repeated.

Bree's face was wet with raindrops and her eyes were shining with curiosity. "This is so cool," she began. "Felicity, our campsite isn't just in a clearing. I think it's in a creek bed!"

"What? Really? How can you tell?" Felicity cried.

"Because there's a stream forming—and it's moving right under Danessa's tent!" Bree said. "This explains those cool, smooth stones we found and everything! The creek bed must've dried up during those hot, sunny days last week, and all this rain has filled it up again."

"Wait a minute. Are you telling me that we're all hanging out in the middle of a creek full of water?" Sage asked. "So instead of being up a creek, we're actually *in* a creek?"

Caper giggled appreciatively at Sage's joke, and the two besties exchanged a high five with their tails.

"That's exactly what I'm trying to say!" Bree replied. "Pretty cool, isn't it? The water is welling up right over the tarps and into the tent."

"Is it dangerous?" Danessa asked. "What if the creek turns into a raging river?"

"I think it would take a lot more rain for this little creek to turn into a river," Bree said. "But it's better to be safe than sorry. We should move to a drier tent."

"I'm sorry about your tent, Danessa," Felicity said. "I had no idea I chose an old creek bed for our campsite."

"That's okay," Danessa replied, Sprint nodding in agreement. "Hey, is anyone looking for some roomies?"

"Sure! You and Sprint can stay in our tent. We'll have a sleepover," Sage offered.

Felicity noticed that Sage hadn't put on her poncho yet—and she had a feeling she knew why. The ponchos, Felicity realized, weren't much use now. They had needed them *before* the storm struck. Underneath their waterproof ponchos, the girls were still drenched and shivering as they crunched on the cold trail mix. Felicity looked from friend to friend as the rain drummed against Danessa's tent. She'd wanted them to have the best camping trip ever, but now they were all cold and wet, with no way to dry off or warm up. They wouldn't even be able to prepare a hot meal to share.

She watched as Patter and Flap huddled together, trying to wring water out of each other's feathers. Felicity knew her friends must be feeling miserable but were far too kind to complain.

Felicity's heart was heavy, but she knew what she had to do. She looked at Flick and could see she was thinking the same thing.

"Yay ya," Flick said sadly.

"I think," Felicity began, "it's time to go home."

CHAPTER SIX

A NEW PLAN

A re you sure?" asked Bree. "I mean, the other tents are on higher ground. They'll probably stay dry inside. At least, I think they will."

"They will stay dry—but we're all wet," Felicity pointed out. "And so is our firewood, and we won't even be able to cook dinner. And poor Patter's and Flap's feathers are completely soaked!"

"Don't worry about us. We'll be okay after a nice hot bath. Tomorrow. When we get home," Patter said.

"Then the sooner you get your bath, the

better," Felicity said. "You deserve it—and with extra bubbles, too!"

Bree pulled the Weather Knower out of her knapsack. The blue light was still blinking rapidly. "It looks as if this storm isn't going away anytime soon," she said.

Danessa turned to Felicity. "If you *really* don't mind calling off the camping trip..." she began.

"Of course I don't mind! It's fine!" Felicity said—almost convincing herself it was true.

Felicity's friends couldn't hide their relief.

"Okay!" Sage said, clapping her hands loudly. "What do we have to do to break down camp, Felicity? Pack up the tents... and then what?"

Felicity waved her hand in the air. "Since it's raining so hard, let's just leave it," she said. "We can come back as soon as the storm ends to break camp. I think the main thing to do right now is grab our knapsacks and *run!*"

"Run, run!" Sprint agreed, scraping his hooves on the ground.

So the friends did just that. The noisy raindrops splattered off leaves and trees, rocks and pinecones, but they weren't loud enough to drown out their shrieks and giggles as they splashed through the puddles on the way back to Wonderwood.

"The first thing I'm going to do when I get home is pull out one of my favorite inventions—it's a fur dryer!" Bree announced. "And then we'll work on our Weather Knower. Wouldn't it be cool if we could predict the weather days—or even weeks—in advance?"

"The first thing I'm going to do is find the thickest, fluffiest towels we have—and then Caper and I are going to wrap up and chill out," Sage said. "Oh, and I'll find the coziest-smelling perfume oil we have to really help us warm up!"

"Chill trick ya do!" Caper added excitedly.

"Of course we can plan some great new pranks when we're all snuggly warm!" Sage said happily.

"Sprint and I are going to brew a nice pot of pine needle tea," Danessa said. "It will be so yummy with the oatcakes I made yesterday."

Felicity, though, was unusually quiet.

"What are you going to do when you get home, Felicity?" Danessa prompted her.

"Me? Oh. I don't know," she replied.

"Dry off, I guess. Make a snack for myself and Flick maybe."

Felicity didn't say anything else until the girls reached the clearing near the heart of Wonderwood. "Sorry the trip was such a disaster," she said, managing a smile. "I'll see you all later."

Then she trudged off toward her home alone, making squelchy footprints in the mud with every step.

The other girls clustered under the thick branches of a pine tree.

"Poor Felicity," Danessa said. "She worked *so* hard to plan this trip."

"All her hard work, ruined because of the rain," Sage added.

"Sad, sad," Caper whispered.

"I don't think I've ever seen her so sad,"

Bree said. "I wish there was something we could do."

Flick nudged Bree's hand. "Hahlah?"

"Yes, I know, Flick," Bree said sympathetically. "It feels awful when someone you care about is upset."

Danessa tilted her head. "Flick, you know Felicity better than anyone else," she began. "Do you have an idea for how we can help Felicity feel better?"

This time, Flick nodded her head up and down, up and down. The answer to Danessa's question was a great, big *yes*!

Danessa knelt down and looked into Flick's eyes. "What are you thinking, Flick?" she asked eagerly. "We all want to help Felicity feel better!"

"Fwends," Flick said firmly.

"Really?" Sage asked. "You think Felicity needs her friends right now?"

"She seemed as if she wanted to be alone," Patter spoke up, looking worried. "She barely said five words as we walked back from the campsite."

"Fwends do da help!" Flick insisted.

"Flick's right," Danessa said. "Felicity needs her friends more than ever right now—and I think I know how we can help her feel better."

"How?" asked Sage.

"Tell us everything!" added Bree.

"Felicity feels sad because she was expecting to spend the whole day and night with her friends at a campout," Danessa explained. "And the rain ruined her plans."

"Go on," Patter encouraged her.

"Well...what if her plans didn't have to

66

change so much after all?" Danessa asked. "What if instead of a campout, we have a camp-*in*?"

Everyone looked surprised by Danessa's suggestion.

"Think about it," she continued. "We'll still be together, doing so many fun things and having such a great time—we'll just be *inside* instead of *outside*."

"I love it!" Bree exclaimed. "We're not going to let a little rain ruin our day!" She and Twist danced around happily.

"It's the perfect plan for cheering up Felicity," Sage declared.

"Ya, ya. We do prank la!" Caper added excitedly.

"That's the spirit, Caper!" Sage replied. "We can definitely come up with a fun prank to help cheer her up!"

"How can we help?" Patter asked. "With the plan, I mean. Let's leave the pranks to Caper and Sage!"

"Here's the plan," Danessa said. "Let's all go home and dry off—then we can get all our supplies together. Bring anything you think we might need for a camp-in. Let's meet at Felicity and Flick's den in one hour."

"It's a plan," Sage declared.

After everyone split up, Flick trotted home to her den. She didn't even notice the splashes of mud that splattered her orange-and-white fur. When Flick returned to the cozy cottage she shared with Felicity, Felicity was waiting for her with a fluffy towel in her hands and a worried look on her face.

"Flick! There you are!" Felicity exclaimed.

"I didn't realize that we got separated on the way back. Where did you go?"

Flick wanted to tell Felicity *everything*—but she didn't want to ruin the surprise. But there was a particular *swish* to Flick's tail as Felicity helped dry her off—and an extra sparkle in her eyes—that caught Felicity's attention.

"You're awfully bright-eyed and bushy-tailed," Felicity said. "It feels good to be warm and dry again, doesn't it?"

And that gave Flick an idea. "Uh-huh! Yep, yep!" she said. Then she grabbed the edge of Felicity's skirt and pulled her toward the hall.

"Whoa!" Felicity said. "What's wrong, Flick?"

"You da go!" Flick replied.

"I guess I *am* pretty muddy," Felicity

replied. "Be right back." Then she slipped into the bathroom and closed the door.

Flick waited until she heard the sound of water running. Then she scampered back to the living room. Flick knew she didn't have much time to start getting ready— and she didn't want to waste a minute of it!

First, Flick moved all the furniture to the far sides of the living room, leaving a big, open space right in the middle. When she was done, it looked a lot like the clearing in the woods—open and inviting but cozy and comfortable at the same time.

What next? Flick paced the length of the living room as she wondered what else she should do to get ready before all their friends arrived.

Tents! she suddenly realized. They'd left their tents back in the clearing, since they were so soggy from the downpour. But Flick and Felicity had shared enough unexpected adventures that Flick knew she could figure something else out instead. She pondered the problem, thoughtfully tapping her paw on the floor.

Then Flick had another bright idea! She dashed over to the closet where Felicity kept all her explorer gear: extra maps, spare binoculars, a compass, backup hiking boots, and more. Flick searched high and low until she found it: a thick coil of rope.

Flick cheered as she pulled the rope back to the living room. She strung it between two chairs, then dragged Felicity's bedspread over it. In no time, Flick had made a cozy little tent for them to share!

"Whoa!" Felicity's voice drifted into the room. "What are you up to, Flick?"

Flick spun around and saw Felicity standing in the doorway. She looked as fresh as the daisies in her hair—but Flick could still sense a heavy cloud of disappointment around her.

But hopefully not for much longer!

"Surprise la!" Flick cried.

Felicity opened her mouth to ask another question, but before she could say anything, there was a knock at the door. Flick was so excited, she bounced back on her hind legs, clapping her paws together.

"I have a feeling you know *exactly* who's at the door," Felicity said. Then she hurried across the room and swung the door wide open. All her friends were scrunched together on the doorstep, just out of the falling rain.

"Surprise!" they exclaimed.

"Where have I heard that before?" Felicity said, giving Flick a knowing look. She held the door open wider and said, "Come in! Hurry! Before you get even wetter!"

Danessa and Sprint, Bree and Twist, Sage and Caper, Patter and Flap: They all streamed into Felicity's den. Their arms were loaded up with boxes and bags, and their cheerful laughter poured throughout Felicity's house like sunshine. For a moment, Felicity was speechless—but only for a moment.

"What—what's everyone doing here?" she asked. "I—we had to cancel the campout. Remember?"

"Of course we remember," Patter said. "That's why we've made plans for a camp-*in*!"

"I don't understand," Felicity replied.

Sage strode across the room and put her hands on Felicity's shoulders. "Listen up, Felicity," she announced. "You did a whole bunch of work to plan an incredible campout for us. And we don't want to miss out on the chance to have an amazing time together just because of a rainstorm!"

"Look at it this way," Patter said. "There will be plenty of pretty days for us to camp outside. But this camp-*in* is a chance to do something special—something different—"

"Something *together*," Danessa added. "Which is the most important thing of all."

Something shifted in Felicity then. Her shoulders went a little straighter, her eyes looked a little brighter, and the smallest hint of a smile flickered across her lips.

"You're totally right!" she agreed. "I'm *so* glad we'll be together after all. I just wish..."

When Felicity's voice trailed off, Sage said, "What do you wish?"

Felicity shrugged. "It's no big deal. It's just kind of hard to have an adventure indoors, you know? I wish we'd gotten to have an adventure together before the storm started and rained us out. I mean— rained us *in*!"

"I wouldn't rule out adventure just yet," Sage spoke up, exchanging a knowing smile with Caper.

Everyone turned to look at her.

"Remember what you've told us so many times?" Sage continued. " 'Adventure is everywhere. Go find it!' "

"That's absolutely right," Felicity said, laughing. "This way to my living room… and our great indoors adventure!"

CHAPTER SEVEN

ANOTHER PERFECT CAMPSITE

As the girls and their besties crowded into Felicity's living room, Felicity turned to Patter. "Feeling better?" she asked.

Patter nodded. "Yes, but I was okay before, too," she said brightly. "I wish our feathers didn't get so soggy and heavy. I guess that's the tradeoff for having such beautiful feathers—they're delicate!"

"Good!" Felicity said. Then she turned

to Flick. "Okay, Flick—you want to tell us what you've been up to in here?"

Flick strode proudly into the middle of the room. "Do la lo *clearing*!" she said as she pranced around the now-open space she had created by moving away all the furniture.

"Just like our special camping spot in the woods. I love it!" Felicity said.

Suddenly, there was a rustle on the other side of the room. The girls froze.

"Wh-what was that?" Patter asked, her words turning into a warbling song.

"In the woods, I'd think it was a squirrel or a chipmunk," Felicity whispered. "But in my living room, with Flick right by my side? I'm not so sure."

The rustling got louder. Then the blanket tent started to move. In a flash of striped fur, Sage and Caper bounded out of the tent. *"BOO!"* they yelled at the same time, making everyone else shriek with excitement.

"How'd you slip away so no one even noticed?" Patter asked, pressing her hand over her heart.

"We can be *very* quiet when we want to be," Sage said, winking at Caper. "After all, some of the best pranks depend on complete and total silence! But enough about that, I want to know how you rigged this great tent. Because I want to build one for myself!"

"Take it away, Flick!" Felicity encouraged her bestie.

Flick showed the girls how she'd strung the rope from different places in the living room, then arranged the blankets over the rope and pinned them down with books. Soon the living room clearing was filled with cozy blanket tents!

"Wow! It almost looks like our campsite in the woods!" Bree marveled.

"It really does," Danessa agreed. "Maybe this will help it feel even more woodsy."

Danessa reached into her knapsack and pulled out stacks of paper leaves. "Sprint and I cut them out of paper," she said. "One of my favorite things about being in the woods is the way the light filters through the trees. The leaves make all kinds of pretty patterns and shadows."

Felicity nodded in agreement. "I love that, too," she replied.

"So, I was trying to figure out a way to

copy that indoors, and I had an idea.... I'm not sure it will work...." Danessa said.

"But it's always worth a try!" Bree exclaimed. "What's your idea?"

Danessa crossed the room to one of the lamps and tacked her leaves to the shade. Sure enough, the light shone around the leaf shapes, casting interesting shadows across the room.

"It works!" Bree cried. "That gives me an idea for an invention...."

"Let's do all the lamps!" Felicity exclaimed. Each girl grabbed a stack of leaves and attached them to the different lampshades in the room while their besties held the lamps steady. Soon Felicity's living room had transformed! The leafy shadows made it look just like a quiet clearing in the forest.

"Well, we've got the woodsy look down," Sage announced. "Now we need to figure out the woodsy *smell*. Check it out!"

She reached into her pocket and pulled out a small amber-colored vial. It had a brass acorn hanging from a slender chain around its stopper.

"*Oooh*, what's that?" Felicity asked, her ears pricking up with interest.

"Caper and I whipped it up," Sage said. "It's maybe, probably, almost certainly our very best scented-oil blend yet. I can't wait for you to smell it! Here—take a whiff!"

Sage carefully uncorked the bottle and waved it near each of her friends. The delicate aroma drifted into the air, a mixture of everything they loved best about the woods: the scent of pine needles and sunshine and blackberries and morning mist, with a touch of moss and wildflowers.

"Wow," Patter breathed. "When I close my eyes, it smells as if I'm right in the middle of the woods. But when I open them..."

"You're right in the middle of our living room!" Felicity said, making everyone laugh. "It's perfect, Sage—how did you do it?"

"A little of this, a little of that," Sage said with a mysterious smile. Caper held up a bundle of felt wildflowers so Sage could add a drop of scented oil to each one. Then the friends scattered the flowers around the room until the scent surrounded them. The floor looked like a meadow in full bloom!

"Light through the leaves? Check," Sage announced. "The great smells of the great outdoors? Check. What else do we need for our camp-in?"

"A campfire!" Bree exclaimed.

Flap looked worried and tugged on Patter's sleeve.

"Don't worry," Patter whispered to her bestie. "Bree knows we can't have a fire in the house. Whatever she's planning will be just as incredible, I bet."

"You do know that, right?" Felicity asked Bree in a low voice. "No campfires in the house?"

Bree laughed. "Of course I do," she said. "But that fireplace of yours will do just fine. Wait until you see my new invention—it will work perfectly over a fireplace"

The girls and their besties watched expectantly as Bree slowly reached into her knapsack. She pulled out several long metal sticks, each with a padded handle at one end. The handles had dials and buttons on them.

"What's that?" Danessa and Patter asked at the same time.

"S'mores roasting sticks! You can program them to whatever speed you want, and they will automatically rotate your marshmallow at the end of the stick! And there's even a sensor that will let you know when your marshmallow has reached the perfect degree of cooked for your personal taste!"

"How does it know what our personal tastes are?" Sage asked curiously.

Bree and Twist danced in excitement. "That's the best part!" Bree replied. "You do the honors, Twist!"

With that, Twist took one of the sticks,

carefully speared a marshmallow on the end, and showed everyone how to set the dial at the end of the stick. The dial had three settings: toasty, super toasty, and ooey-gooey extra toasty.

Her friends burst into applause. "So cool!" Felicity exclaimed.

After the fireplace was lit, Bree and Twist handed out the roasting sticks to everyone. Before long, everyone had chosen his or her perfect setting, and the marshmallow roasting was underway!

"You know what else we can do while we're roasting our marshmallows over our 'campfire,' though?" Patter asked excitedly. "Sing! *La-la-la-la-la!*"

As usual, Patter's voice was off-key, but when Flap chimed in, they made the perfect duo, singing in beautiful harmony.

The other girls and their besties sang along as Patter and Flap taught them some fun new campfire songs.

"I have one more surprise," Bree said. "A brand-new invention...so new, I've never even tested it out before. I really hope it works!"

"What is it? What is it?" her friends asked eagerly.

Bree smiled as she pulled a glittery silver box out of her knapsack. "It's...a star shooter!" she exclaimed.

"Whoa!"

"Cool!"

"Wow!"

Everyone was talking at once, but Bree didn't mind. "I was really excited when Felicity said we might even see shooting stars. But of course, we can't see them with so many clouds in the sky. So I thought an indoor star shooter would be the next best thing!"

"How does it work?" Sage asked.

"I've filled it with glow-in-the-dark paper stars," Bree explained. "Theoretically, when I push the button, the star shooter should send them flying all around the room! But like I said, I haven't tested it yet. Who knows if it will work... or not... or do something totally unexpected and surprising!"

"Ooh, sounds *very* exciting," Patter said.

"What do you think?" Bree asked. "Should we give it a try?"

"Yes! Yes! Yes!" her friends chorused.

Bree flipped the switch to power up her star shooter. Then she took a deep breath moved her finger toward the gold button.

"Wait!" Patter suddenly cried out.

Everyone turned to look at her.

"The lights!" she continued. "You said the stars glow, right? So we should turn out the lights to make sure we can see them even better!"

"Of course!" Felicity exclaimed. "Why didn't I think of that?"

Quick as a wink, Felicity and Flick dashed around the room, snapping off each light in their den. *Click. Click. Click.*

"Now we're ready," Patter said with a satisfied smile. "Go for it, Bree!"

"Hope it works," Bree said, crossing her fingers. Twist even crossed her ears for luck! Then Bree pressed the gold button and waited expectantly.

Whoosh!

Whoosh!

Whoosh!

Almost immediately, gleaming stars burst from the star shooter! Felicity shrieked with glee. Bree's shooting stars were almost as unexpected and breathtaking as the real thing!

"I'm going to catch a star!" Felicity cried, jumping as high as she could whenever a star *zinged* overhead. "Now, that's something you can't do with a real shooting star!"

Soon the darkened room was glowing softly from all the beautiful stars that Bree's star shooter had launched. They were on the chairs and the sofa, the bookshelf and the floor, the tents and the table. The girls and their besties chased after the enchanting stars until they collapsed, breathless and giggling, onto a stack of leaf-shaped pillows.

"That was so fun!" Danessa said as she and Sprint touched their antlers together happily.

"Watching for shooting stars doesn't usually take so much energy," Felicity replied. "I'm hungry!"

"Me too," Sage agreed.

"Hey, look," Bree said as she glanced out the window. "It's dark outside!"

"Wow, you're right," Patter said. "I didn't even notice—the stars are glowing so brightly in here."

CHAPTER EIGHT

ADVENTURE IS EVERYWHERE

After dinner, Felicity and her pals returned to their campsite in the living room. The fireplace campfire was still glowing softly, along with the stars. Felicity almost turned on the lights but stopped herself just in time. *If we were really camping in the woods, we couldn't just turn on the lights when it got dark*, she reminded herself.

"What are you thinking?"

Felicity jumped a little. In the darkness,

she hadn't noticed that Danessa had joined her.

"Oh!" Felicity exclaimed. "It's silly—I almost turned on the lights before I realized that if it would be dark on a real camping trip, we should keep it dark in here, too."

"That makes sense," Danessa said, nodding. "I'm having such a great time, Felicity. I know it's not the same as camping in the woods, but I'm so glad we're all together."

"Me too," Felicity replied—and she truly meant it. The indoor camping trip was better than she'd imagined it could be, even if it didn't really have much adventure. Felicity's smile turned wistful. *I wish I could've given my friends the chance to have an amazing adventure today*, she thought.

Then, Felicity paused, mid-step. Sage's

words—the same words Felicity herself had said so many times—rang through her memory.

Adventure is everywhere. Go find it!

From all her wild and wonderful experiences exploring the world with Flick, Felicity knew that it was true.

So why shouldn't Felicity find adventure in her very own living room?

Felicity's eyes twinkled as brightly as the fireplace campfire. "Come on, everybody!" she cried. "Let's sit around the campfire."

"Are we going to sing more songs?" Sage asked with a glance toward Patter.

"Actually, I was thinking we could tell stories!" Felicity announced. "Stories around a crackling campfire is one of my favorite camping traditions. And I had an idea, too—instead of telling lots of different stories, we could tell one extra-special one, us all together."

"How could we all tell the same story?" Patter asked, confused.

"We're going to build one...together," Felicity said. She scanned the room for the biggest star from Bree's star shooter and grabbed it. "Whoever holds this star is the storyteller. When you finish your part, throw it to someone else. Then it's *her* turn to tell the story, picking up right where you left off!"

"*Ooh*, sounds cool," Danessa said. "I've never told a story like that before."

"Neither have I," Felicity said. "That's all part of the adventure! Who wants to go first?"

"*You* should go first!" Bree said. "It's your great idea."

"Yeah! You'll get our story started right," Sage added.

Felicity grinned at her friends. "Okay!" she replied. "Just give me one minute...." Then she leaned over and whispered something in Flick's ear. Flick scratched her chin, deep in thought, then whispered something back to Felicity. "That's perfect, Flick!" the fox-girl exclaimed, waggling ears with her bestie.

"Okay, here we go: Once upon a time, there was a girl named...Olivia...who lived on the top of a mountain. One day, a storm came. Not just any storm, though. A big, loud, terrible, *horrible* storm, where the rain poured down and the thunder went *BOOM*!"

As Felicity yelled "BOOM," she clapped her hands so loudly that everyone jumped.

"No one could go outside for days. No—weeks!" she continued. "The rain turned tiny streams into raging rivers. Hills became islands. And just when Olivia thought the storm would never stop..."

Felicity could tell that her friends were waiting breathlessly for the next part of the story. Without warning, she tossed the star to Danessa. It landed in Danessa's lap. She was so startled that she froze for a moment, until Sprint gave her a gentle nudge.

"My turn? Now?" Danessa exclaimed. "You want *me* to go on with the story?"

Felicity nodded. "Go for it!" she replied.

Danessa took a deep breath. "And just when Olivia *thought* the storm would never stop...it did."

Felicity's face fell. *That's it?* she

wondered. *That wasn't much of an adventure story. It wasn't even much of a regular story.* And she wasn't the only one who felt that way.

"Danessa!" Sage said in a loud whisper. "Whatever happens next is supposed to be exciting!"

"I know, Sage!" Danessa replied. "Be patient! I'm getting to the good part!"

"Oops. Sorry," Sage said. "Go ahead."

"Olivia was so glad that the terrible storm was over," Danessa continued. "She couldn't wait to wander down to the meadow and pick some—some—some—"

"Blueberries?" suggested Patter.

Danessa flashed her a grateful smile. "Yes! Blueberries! For her breakfast!" Danessa said. "But as soon as she stepped outside, Olivia heard a terrible—horrible—*scary* noise!"

Everyone gasped!

"What was it?" Bree exclaimed as Twist leaped into her arms.

"It was—it sounded like—" Danessa began. Then a mischievous smile crossed her face as she tossed the star to Sage.

"Oh!" Sage exclaimed in surprise. "I mean, it sounded like—*ohhhwoooooooooooooo! Ohhhwoooooooooooooooo!*"

"What was it?" Felicity whispered.

"That's practically what Olivia said," Sage answered. " 'What was that?' It was the spookiest, creepiest sound that she'd ever heard. Ever!"

"So what did she do?" Bree asked.

"Olivia didn't know *what* to do," Sage said.

"Should she skip berry picking? Run back inside? Hide under her bed? Every so often, she'd hear it again: *Ohhhwoooooooooooooooo!*"

"*Ahhhhh!*" everyone screamed.

Sage paused dramatically. "Or... should Olivia investigate?"

"Investigate!" all the other girls yelled at the same time.

"Olivia thought and thought and thought. It was the hardest decision ever! At last, Olivia knew what to do." Then Sage smiled and tossed the star to Bree.

"My turn!" Bree exclaimed. "Olivia had to investigate, of course. She *had* to find out what was making that noise! She got her detective kit—"

"Olivia is a detective?" Patter whispered to Felicity.

"She is now!" Felicity whispered back.

"And set off down the mountain to find out who—or what—was going *Ohhhwooooooooooooooo!*" Bree said. "She tiptoed along the trail, not making a single sound. Except her footprints in the mud made a funny squishing sound."

"Like this?" Sage asked. She pursed her lips and made a squishy, sucking noise that made all her friends laugh.

"Yes! Exactly like that!" Bree said. "Olivia was worried that her footsteps would give her away to whoever—or whatever—was making that noise."

"*Ohhhwooooooooooooooooooo!*" Sage added.

"I nominate Sage to be in charge of sound effects," Felicity said.

"Come on, let Bree get back to the

story!" Patter cried. "I want to know what happens next!"

Bree glanced at Sage. "Will you do the sound effects for me?"

"Sure!" she said.

"So Olivia was hiking down the trail—"

"Squish-squash-squelch—"

"And the strange noise was getting louder—"

"Ohhwooooooooooooooooooooo!"

"And louder—"

"Ohhhhhhhhhhhhhhhhhhhhhwoooooooooooo-oooooooooooooooooooo!"

"And even louder!"

"OHHHHHHHHHHHHHHHHHHHHWOO-OOOOOOOOOOOOOOOOOOOOOOOOO-OOOOOO!"

"Until at last, Olivia came to the old

oak, the tallest tree in the forest. But now, it was surrounded by water—like a tree island! And the water was getting higher and higher and—"

Bree paused to toss the star to Patter.

"And—and—and Olivia heard the noise again!" Patter said breathlessly. Beside her, Flap fluttered around in excitement

"*Ohhhwoooooooooooooooo,*" Sage said, right on cue.

"She looked up," Patter said, "and saw, on the tippy-top of the tallest branch, an itty-bitty baby *owl*!"

"*Awwww!*" the girls cried. Flick nuzzled Felicity's hand.

"But the owl was up so high that it didn't know how to get down," Patter continued. "Especially with the tree surrounded by so much water!"

"Couldn't it just fly down from the tree?" Sage asked.

"No!" Patter said loudly. "The baby owl *couldn't* fly, because its feathers were all waterlogged from the big storm!" she explained. "They were so soggy and heavy that the baby owl was *trapped*!"

The girls and their besties waited breathlessly to find out what would happen next.

"Olivia knew she had to rescue the little owl—even though it was so high up," Patter said. "But how could she get to the tippy-top of the old oak when she didn't have wings?"

Patter's face went blank, as if she couldn't answer her own question. Then, in one fast movement, she tossed the star back to Felicity.

"Luckily, Olivia's detective kit had everything she needed for the biggest climb of her life!" Felicity said without missing a beat. "And for more detail on what was in her kit—" Felicity tossed the star to Bree.

Twist caught the star and handed it to Bree. Bree took a deep breath and continued the story. "Olivia tossed a rope up to one of the branches, then tied it around her waist. She used the magnifying glass to examine the tree trunk before she started to climb. And then, hand over hand, she went up, up, up, *up*!"

"Hooray!" all the friends exclaimed.

Bree handed the star back to Twist, who tossed it to Felicity so she could finish the story.

"The baby owl was so happy to see Olivia that she hopped right into her arms,"

Felicity continued. "Then they climbed down the old oak and . . . picked a basketful of blueberries to share . . . and lived happily ever after."

Everyone started clapping.

"That story was incredible!" Sage said. "I had no idea what was going to happen next!"

"I don't think any of us did," Patter said, making everyone laugh.

"Who knew that hearing about an adventure could be just as exciting as having one?" Felicity asked. "This camp-in has been full of surprises!"

CHAPTER NINE

SWEET DREAMS

After the girls finished their s'mores, Sage yawned loudly. "It must be getting pretty late, huh?"

"Yeah...I'm sleepy," Patter replied.

"Um, so are Twist and Caper," Bree whispered, pointing to her bestie, sound asleep in front of the fire with Caper sleeping right next to her. As if Twist had heard her name, she stretched out in her sleep and let out a big *snore,* which somehow didn't even make Caper stir. The friends laughed.

"PJ time?" asked Felicity.

"Definitely," Sage replied, covering her mouth as she yawned again.

Bree gathered Twist in a cozy blanket, and Sage did the same for Caper. Then the girls slipped into their tents with their besties cuddled up next to them.

"Good night," everyone whispered in the darkness. "Sweet dreams!"

Soon the only sound in the room was a low humming from Patter and Flap, a gentle harmony that was the most soothing lullaby Felicity had ever heard. She was tired, too. It had been such a long day; it felt like a lifetime ago that she and Flick had set up the first campsite in the clearing that became a creek. That was before the s'mores maker, before the camp-in, before the storm, before the bad-weather warnings from Bree's Weather Knower.... It was so funny now, how Felicity had wanted everything to be so perfect. Nothing had gone exactly to plan, and yet the day had turned out even better than she'd dreamed.

I guess there was more adventure today than I realized, Felicity thought, smiling to herself. *The best kind of adventure, too—the kind you share with your friends.*

Soon even Patter and Flap's song faded into silence. Everyone was asleep.

Everyone except Felicity and Flick.

Felicity rolled over, trying to get comfortable so she could fall asleep at last. As she turned onto her side, though, something caught her eye through the window.

It was the moon, shining brightly in the night sky.

The moon! Felicity thought excitedly. If

she could see the moon, that meant the clouds had broken. Maybe, just maybe, the big storm was finally over. Maybe the sun would be shining when they awoke the next morning, helping to dry their tents before they packed them up. Maybe, just maybe, they could explore the secret path after all!

Being extra careful to be extra quiet, Felicity crawled out of her sleeping bag for a better look. Flick, like always, was right by her side. Felicity stroked Flick's silky fur, feeling the fox's warmth on her fingers as they silently admired the gleaming moon.

Then—suddenly—a streak of light came flashing through the night sky!

It was over almost as suddenly as it began, but Felicity knew what she and Flick had just seen. "A shooting star," she whispered close to Flick's ear. "Make a wish!"

GET ENCHANTED

Journey to a fantastical world with the
Enchantimals and their animal besties,
where fun and adventure are
right around every corner!